THE GROSSERY GANG

YOUR SHOPPiN'S GONE ROTTEN!

A ROTTEN EASTER!

SIZZLE PRESS

"Today is Easter," Crusty Chocolate Bar said to the rest of the Grossery Gang.

"Ah, Easter," sighed Blue Spew Cheese. "I remember those toxic Easter egg hunts and how we all used to love rolling down the garbage chute for the Easter race."

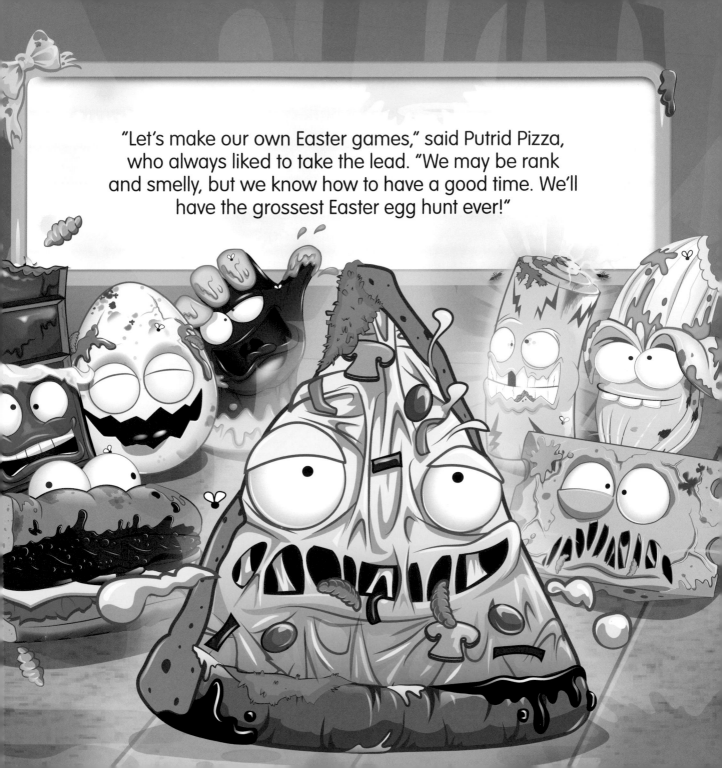

"Let's make our own Easter games," said Putrid Pizza, who always liked to take the lead. "We may be rank and smelly, but we know how to have a good time. We'll have the grossest Easter egg hunt ever!"

"There's one problem," said Flat Battery as he leaked toxic gunk.
"We don't have any Easter eggs at the Yucky Mart.
What are we going to hide?"

The others agreed that this was indeed a problem.
But then, one by one, they slowly turned
toward Rotten Egg.

"What are you all looking at?" Rotten Egg asked nervously, releasing a horrible gas.

"You can be our Easter egg," Putrid Pizza explained. "Your orange slime is just as tasty as chocolate! Now run and hide, Rotten Egg, and we'll all try to find you!"

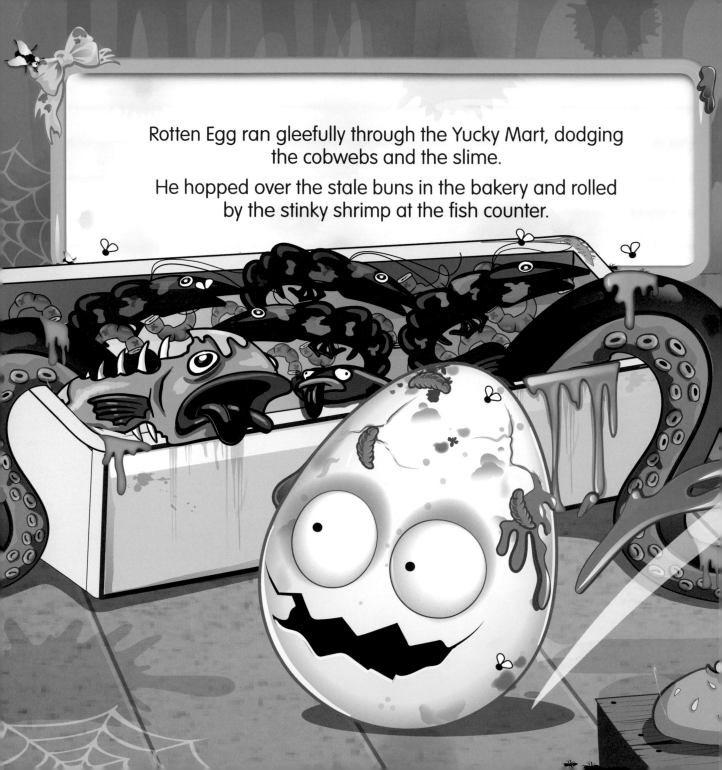

Rotten Egg ran gleefully through the Yucky Mart, dodging the cobwebs and the slime.

He hopped over the stale buns in the bakery and rolled by the stinky shrimp at the fish counter.

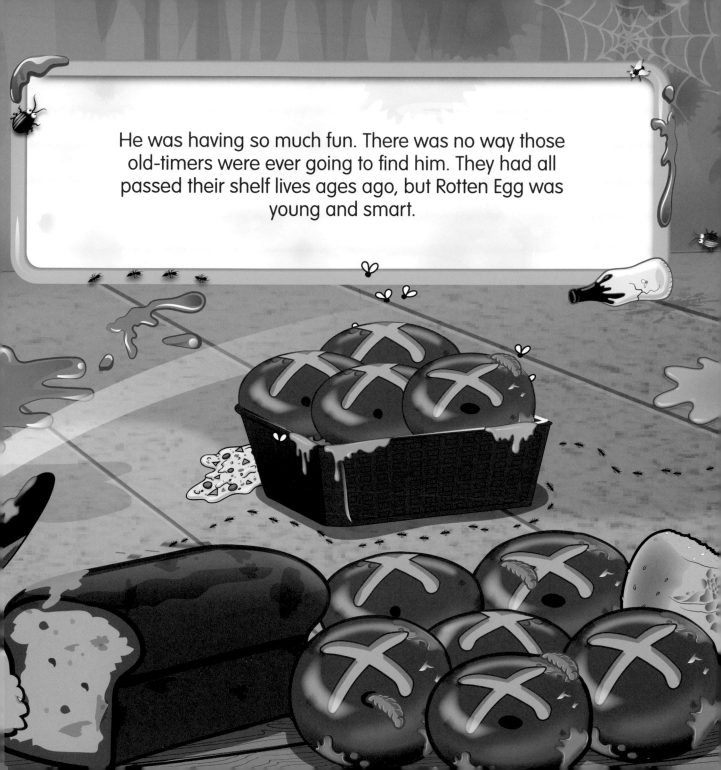

He was having so much fun. There was no way those old-timers were ever going to find him. They had all passed their shelf lives ages ago, but Rotten Egg was young and smart.

Still chuckling at how easily he had outsmarted his friends, Rotten Egg rolled his way to the rusty escalator. It hadn't worked for years, but that was no problem. He decided to do an egg roll.

Rotten Egg thought that rolling eggs down a hill was something everyone did at Easter, so he got ready to roll.

"Here I go!" he chuckled to himself as he leapt off the top of the escalator. "Whee!" he yelled as he tumbled down.

Rotten Egg giggled all the way down the escalator. He bumped his head a lot and lost quite a bit of his shell, but he didn't mind. More cracks meant he'd ooze a lot more fabulous, yucky goo!

He rolled all the way to the Yucky Mart's old fountain.
Anyone could smell that thick, brown, sludgy water
from miles away.

"That was fun!" Rotten Egg said to himself. He decided
to do another egg roll and turned toward the escalator.
Suddenly, his eyes widened with horror.

As he looked back, Rotten Egg saw that he had left a thin trail of sticky yolk all the way down the escalator. The orange goo was on every step. It continued off the steps onto the floor and led right up to the fountain.

"I must have left that sludge trail wherever I went!" he wailed. "The bakery, the fish counter, EVERYWHERE. The others are going to find me in no time!"

Poor Rotten Egg was right.

"This is so easy," Flat Battery scoffed as he led the others down the escalator, following Rotten Egg's trail of sticky yolk. "That cracked-up egg didn't even think to cover his tracks."

"That's the trouble with kids," said Putrid Pizza. "They're just not as smart as they think they are!"

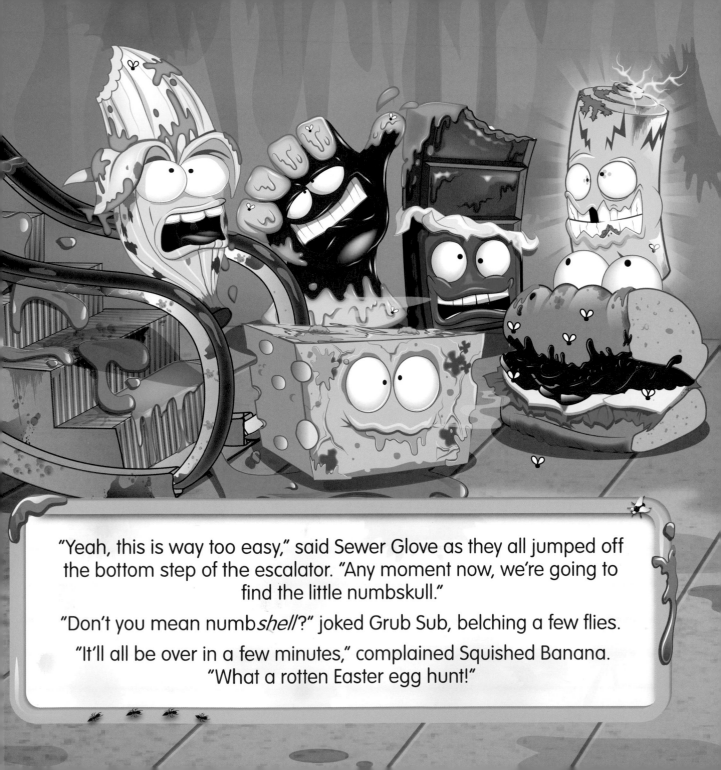

"Yeah, this is way too easy," said Sewer Glove as they all jumped off the bottom step of the escalator. "Any moment now, we're going to find the little numbskull."

"Don't you mean numb*shell*?" joked Grub Sub, belching a few flies.

"It'll all be over in a few minutes," complained Squished Banana. "What a rotten Easter egg hunt!"

The gang quickly reached the old fountain, but suddenly, the yolk trail just stopped.

"I don't get it," said Sewer Glove, scratching his head with two of his icky green fingers.

"Maybe Rotten Egg is smarter than we thought," said Putrid Pizza. He pointed at the fountain's deep, brown water, which had a foul green froth floating on top. "He could have dunked himself in here, so he wouldn't leave a trail of runny yolk wherever he went."

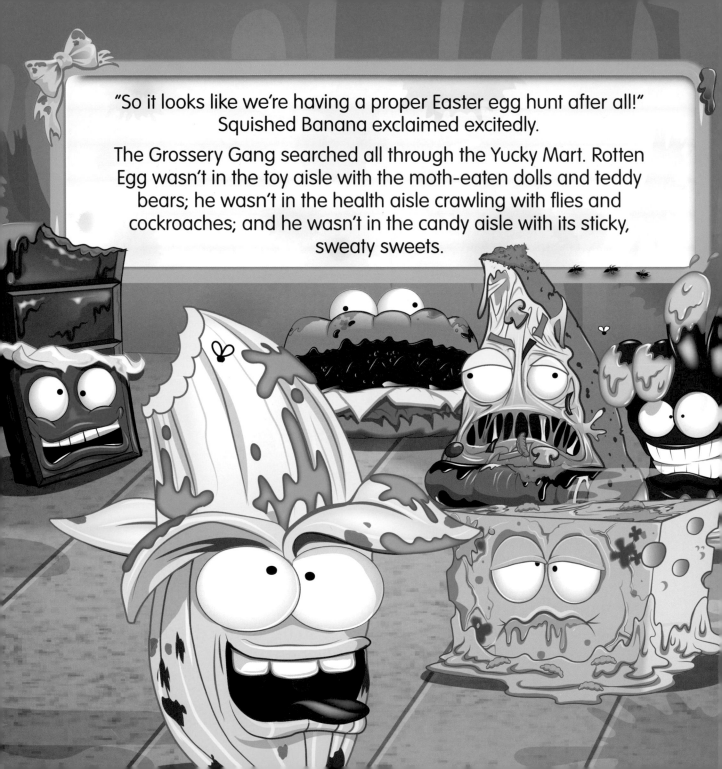

"So it looks like we're having a proper Easter egg hunt after all!" Squished Banana exclaimed excitedly.

The Grossery Gang searched all through the Yucky Mart. Rotten Egg wasn't in the toy aisle with the moth-eaten dolls and teddy bears; he wasn't in the health aisle crawling with flies and cockroaches; and he wasn't in the candy aisle with its sticky, sweaty sweets.

"I'm exhausted," said Flat Battery, feeling even flatter than usual.

"Me, too," said Grub Sub, panting and dribbling maggoty ketchup. "This Easter egg hunt is really hard."

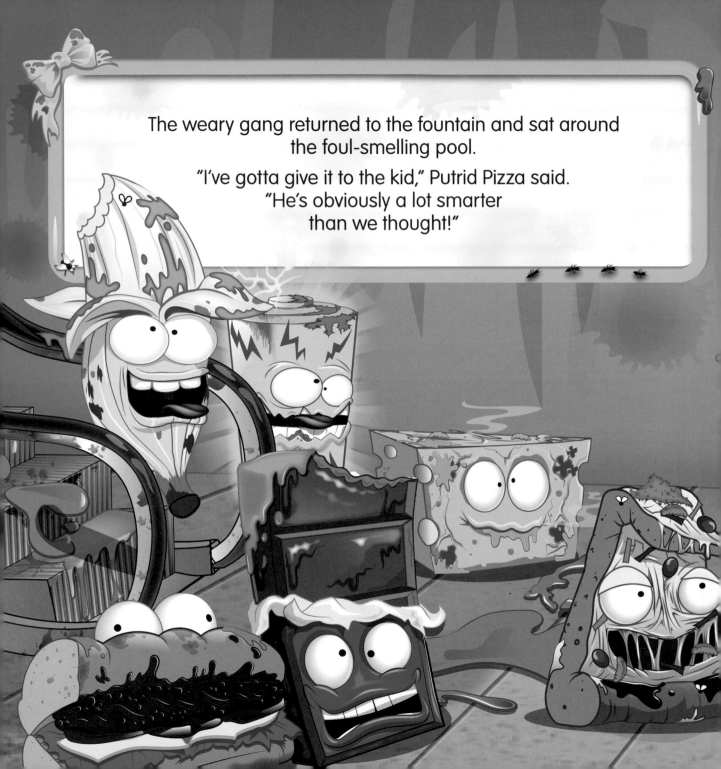

"Aha!" blurted Rotten Egg as he jumped out of the pool's murky depths with a sudden *whoosh*. "It's nice to be out of all that yucky water. I don't think I could have held my breath for a second longer!"

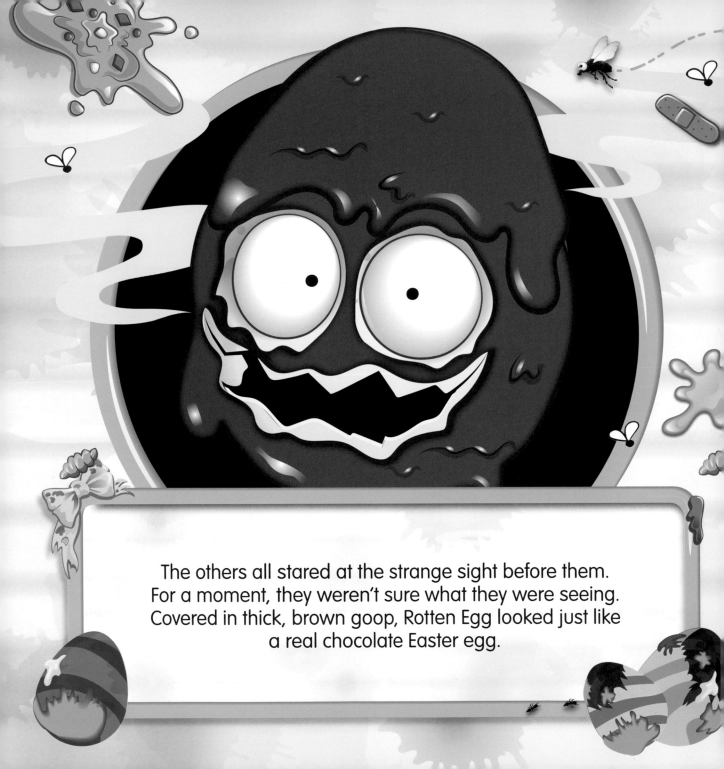

The others all stared at the strange sight before them.
For a moment, they weren't sure what they were seeing.
Covered in thick, brown goop, Rotten Egg looked just like
a real chocolate Easter egg.

The muddy water dripped off of Rotten Egg, revealing his cracked smile.

"Egghead, is that you?" asked Putrid Pizza.

"You bet!" said Rotten Egg. "I tricked you all!"

Everyone started laughing.

"Good job, Egghead," said Putrid Pizza. "This was the funniest, best, and grossest Easter egg hunt ever!"